THE BEAST

MONSTERS AND BEAUTIES

JENIKA SNOW

THE BEAST (Monsters and Beauties)

By Jenika Snow

www.JenikaSnow.com

Jenika_Snow@Yahoo.com

Copyright © June 2022 by Jenika Snow

First E-book and Paperback Publication: June 2022

Cover Designer: Haya in Designs

Editors: Snow Queen Editing

Beta Readers: Judy Ann Loves Books

Proof Reader: Jill Reading

CHAPTER
ONE

Belle

My father had just sold me off. Bartered my body to erase his debt to the very devil himself.

A Beast of a man. Literally.

A creature whispered about amongst the villagers, feared by all, and known to have immense wealth and power that no one could ever conceivably stand up against.

I knew only a handful had ever seen him, but I heard the rumors of his appearance.

A beastly visage at three times the size of a man, and his monstrously huge body covered in fur. His eyes held an unearthly red glow, and his pawlike hands were tipped with claws. Then there were his fangs, ones that I wondered if he used to tear into flesh.

I visibly shivered at the image my mind conjured up.

I held in my tears as I clenched my hands tightly into fists. Anger, fear, and shock waged war in me.

"Don't look at me like that, Belle. I didn't have a choice."

I had to give my father credit... he at least looked heartbroken.

"You always have a choice. How could you just give me away like that? And *to him?*" I hissed out the last part.

His shoulders sagged and he dropped his head, exhaling as if it were his life that was being ruined.

"We would have lost everything. The little land we own, our home, the livestock..." He looked at me. "We would have been penniless and out in the streets."

"It would have been better than marrying that... that *Beast*." I turned from my father, unable to look at him anymore.

It was no secret in the village that my father had a gambling addiction. He owed too many people money. He had far too many debts to ever be repaid in our lifetime.

And it finally caught up with him.

"Gaston wouldn't wait for me to pay him back this time, Belle," my father pleaded, trying to pull on my heartstrings.

Not this time. There had been too many instances where I'd had to bend over backward to fix his mistakes, where I had to use the little savings I had to pay off the debtors who'd come by.

I'd had to work extra at the village seamstress to make a few additional coins for food because he'd spent all our money gambling. My fingers had bled because I'd worked and tried so hard.

"We would have lost everything," he whispered pitifully again.

I was done with it all. *Because I don't have a choice anymore.*

"Instead, I'm losing my freedom."

I turned from him and told myself a proper lady didn't act this way. But I'd never been so hurt and angry in my life.

"They were going to take everything, and then they were going to kill me, Belle. Kill me right in the tavern last night with a handful of villagers as witnesses if I didn't pay up."

I looked at him with what I knew was a horrified expression. The silence stretched out, neither one of us able to speak after those heavy words were spoken and hung in the air between us.

"You dug yourself too deep this time." I pinched the bridge of my nose with my thumb and forefinger and exhaled. I was tired. So tired.

"I'm sorry."

I knew he was, but then again, he was always sorry when the journey was too hard to take.

"I don't even understand how you were propositioned for something like this."

"One of his men was at the tavern. He overheard what was happening and said he'd pay the debt, wipe the slate clean if I agreed to what he wanted in return." My father had the nerve to glance away, his shame surrounding him. "I agreed wholeheartedly before I knew what he wanted."

I wasn't embarrassed to admit I thought about running, slipping out in the night and escaping. But as I looked at my father, knowing they'd kill him slowly because I wasn't here to once again clean up his mess, any thoughts of leaving him to the proverbial wolves flew out the door.

"How long do I have?" The words were pushed out through gritted teeth. When he didn't respond, I looked at him. The discomfort on his face was tangible. "How long?"

He swallowed and looked at the flames burning in the hearth. "A fortnight."

The air wheezed out of me and I braced a hand on the table.

A fortnight before I was given to a Beast who would no doubt use me in every deplorable, animalistic and primal way he saw fit.

CHAPTER
TWO

Belle

His home was a castle, sitting atop a massive mountain, the weather making it seem frightening and other-worldly.

My new home.

The rain and wind whipped by me so fiercely it stung any bared part of my skin.

I wrapped my cloak around my body and tilted my head back to look up at the mansion that stood ominously before me.

A crack of lightning arched across the sky, momentarily flashing in the background and showcasing the gargoyles sitting devilishly on corbels at each corner of the castle.

I swallowed the lump of fear lodged in my throat as I tightened my hand around the strap of my lone satchel. The contents contained the few items of importance I owned.

A glance over my shoulder showed the carriage was gone, no longer even a mirage in the foggy, misty distance of the long, winding property.

I'd been picked up at our cottage as soon as the sun had set over the horizon. The coachman had taken my bag, gestured me into the carriage, and ever since then I'd been moving in a hazy-like state.

The long, stone-covered, tree-lined approach to the estate was frighteningly empty, with a gray hue settled over it and the rain pouring down with unrelenting anger.

With a steady inhale followed by an exhale, I made my way up the stone steps. One of the bolt-studded doors opened on its own before I got to it, and my heart doubled in rhythm.

I didn't know what I expected to find, but it wasn't the older woman who stood right inside the entryway, her black-and-white livery outfit pressed and formed around her curvy body.

Her gray and white hair was pulled up into a

tight bun, and the smile she gave me was warm and friendly.

No, she certainly wasn't what I expected to find.

"Welcome, welcome, welcome." She clapped her hands and pressed them to her ample bosom as she looked me up and down. "Aren't you quite the sight? The Master of the estate chose well."

I wasn't sure what she meant by that. We'd never seen each other, so how did he "choose well"?

"Thank you?" I hadn't meant to phrase that like a question. I stepped inside, and a second later the heavy door closed behind me with a resounding echo.

I jumped, startled as I whirled around to see a candlestick-thin man in the same livery attire looking at me with a warm smile.

He was younger, his dark blond hair slicked back, and when he welcomed me, I could hear a thick accent, one from a distant land.

"I am Madame." The older woman gestured to herself then pointed to the man behind me. "This is Pierre. He handles any and all housekeeping around the house." She clapped her hands again and gestured me farther inside. "But we have lots of time to go into more of that. You must be weary and famished from your travel."

Pierre took my bag before I knew what he was doing, startling me once again. And then I was being ushered through the grand foyer. I'd never seen so much wealth and opulence.

I followed her up the wide staircase, the carpeting beneath my feet plush, making my steps soundless.

She kept chatting away and explaining all the different artifacts hanging on the walls and the vases on podiums. But my mind was blank, my body just following the motions and orders.

I wasn't absorbing anything, and I wondered if I was in shock, but the numbness was welcome.

Finally, when we got to one of the rooms at the end of the elaborately long hallway, she pushed the door open and I stepped inside, shock once again encompassing me.

The room was exquisite, with a large four-poster bed pressed against one wall, a grand fireplace across from it, a vanity with trinkets and knick-knacks sitting on the marble top, and silk adorning the windows.

The color scheme was a light blue-and-gray ensemble that seemed to make the room appear gentler and not at all like my new prison. And after my shock slowly started to wane, I felt completely out of place.

"The wardrobe is over here," Madame said and pointed to the elaborate, carved armoire. She pulled it open to show the interior contents, with gowns and dresses of gorgeous colors and expensive material.

I found myself reaching out and running my fingers along a particularly beautiful gown with flower embroidery in perfect detail.

"Master has picked out each piece. He has impeccable taste and knew just the things to get you so they would accentuate your natural beauty."

I glanced at Madame and felt my throat tighten. I didn't know what to think about the Beast hand-selecting anything, especially gowns as delicate and exquisite as the ones that were now mine.

"The lavatories are through that door."

I was thankful she changed the subject as she pointed to a door in the corner.

"Dinner will be ready at half past six. Master has requested your attendance." The way she said that last part had me bristling, as if I wasn't to even think of disobeying. Not that I would. I'd willingly come here, knew my role, and wouldn't change my mind.

My father may have put me in horrible positions over and over again throughout my life, but he was the only family I had left, and throwing him to the wolves to save my own skin wasn't in my nature.

"Master has also selected your dinner attire." She gestured to the bed, where a large white box tied with a red satin ribbon sat atop the lush mattress.

I'd been so stunned by everything that I hadn't noticed it at first.

With one more smile she left me alone, closing the door behind her.

For a second I was frozen in place, my knees threatening to buckle, but I closed my eyes and breathed out slowly.

I was now legally bound to the man—the Beast —they called Master. Forms had been signed before I'd been picked up to be taken to my new home. My father had apologized repeatedly, but I'd been in too much of a fog to pay attention to him or what he said.

How could I pay attention to anything but being legally bound to my new husband—his will something I had to bend to, submit to?

I only allowed ten minutes of alone time to compose myself. I wanted to cry, scream, break something, and just get the frustration out, but I knew none of that would help me right now.

And refusing wasn't an option, not when my father's life was at stake.

This all seemed like a dream, with the expensive things, the lavish attendance, and the waitstaff serving me hand and foot. But I wasn't a fool in knowing what this reality really was about.

I'd read the paperwork before I signed it.

This wasn't just the Beast needing a wife. He wanted heirs.

THREE

Belle

I tightened my hands around the skirting of the dress the Beast had picked out for me to wear for dinner tonight.

It was a soft blue with a yellow satin ribbon tied under the bust. The sleeves were dainty and capped, and my neck, shoulders, and most of my arms were exposed.

I was dressed but somehow felt bare.

I was about to step out of the room and go downstairs when Madame arrived and instantly eyed me. She *tsked* as she came to stop before me and lifted a lock of my long brown hair.

"This won't do. Master requested your hair up

and out of the way."

Out of the way for what, exactly?

She said it so matter-of-factly that I was too stunned to speak and just stood there as she expertly tied my hair into a chignon at the crown of my head.

With a few more fusses to my dress, and after she applied another generous swipe of red lipstick to my lips, she ushered me out of the room.

I felt as if I were in a fog as we descended the long, ornate staircase and I was led into the grand dining room.

The table sat in the center of the room, long and lavishly dressed with candelabras lit, crystal and porcelain dishware, and large, dome-covered silver platters hiding the food underneath.

There were bowls of fresh fruit, cut cheeses, freshly baked rolls, squares of butter on tiny gold-leaf plates, and wine goblets sat at the place settings.

The fireplace mantel was grand, double my size in height and width, a fire intimately crackling and throwing light and shadow throughout the entire room. The crystal chandelier that hung above the table cast prisms of rainbows across the room.

This certainly hadn't been what I envisioned of

the Beast's home. I'd pictured dank and dark living quarters, mold-infested walls, and steel-barred cells I'd call home.

I hadn't expected such... beauty.

Maybe the rumors I'd heard of my new husband were false? Maybe he wasn't some ugly, horrid Beast that I'd have to sleep with. Maybe he was a gorgeous prince with flowing golden locks and gentle blue eyes who wanted us to get to know each other before we consummated the marriage.

"Master will be here momentarily. Per his request, dinner and wine are already set and waiting. Staff have been sent away for the evening."

My throat once again tightened at the prospect of being alone with him, my anxiety filling every recess of my body.

I knew the moment Madame had left, when everyone was cleared out of the castle. Because I felt an instant, sudden hollowness surrounding me to the point it was almost crushing.

I was used to being alone, what with my father and his provocations that left me at the house. But at least I'd been around creature comforts, things that made me happy, that didn't make me feel terrified to even breathe.

I'd never been somewhere that was so big or

grand or lavish.

I was lost in my thoughts when I heard the first sounds come through the large expanse of the room. At first I wasn't sure what it was, and I turned to face the entrance of the room.

Thump. Thump. Thump.

My heart started fluttering harder, and I gathered the fall of my dress, tightening my fingers until they ached.

The sound grew closer, and I realized what it was.

Footsteps.

He was coming for me.

I held my breath and took a step back just as the Beast finally made his appearance.

That one step back wasn't enough for what I was looking at, for how the very instinctual part of me said to escape.

I found myself stumbling back as the Beast—the monster and my new husband—stepped into the dining hall. The rumors of him had been true.

He was utterly terrifying.

Easily three times the size of a human man, with shoulders terrifyingly broad, and a barreled chest that blocked out everything behind him.

His massive biceps and forearms were hairy, but

even that couldn't hide the power in them. And his face... completely inhuman.

He had a wide forehead, pitch-black eyes, and a nose that reminded me of a primal animal. And his legs—God, they appeared to be like a feline, or even of the canine variety, bent oddly and tipped with massive paws.

His hair was dark and fell to his shoulders, only broken up by the huge, arcing horns that curved back and away from his forehead.

And his mouth was full and wide, his teeth sharp, and the lower ones like daggers. My heart thundered as I stared at them which looked more like tusks than teeth, protruding up so that when he closed his mouth, they were still frighteningly visible.

He wore clothing fit for a noble, but it couldn't hide how animalistic and utterly primal he was.

Nothing could mask how entirely terrifying he was.

He took a step forward, and another one, and I swore I felt the floor vibrate from the force. His legs and feet reminded me of the illustrations from fairy tales about the werewolves that prowled the dark, danger-filled forests, walking on their hind legs. Paws... God, he had black, claw-tipped paws.

His focus was already trained on me. He looked like the very devil himself.

I made sure to keep the table between us, although I knew it was foolish. This was just cloth and wood, glass and steel. It wouldn't keep a creature like him away from something he wanted, even if right now I felt like this piece of furniture could hold back a demon such as himself.

He didn't speak and neither did I, my tongue in knots as I watched him come farther into the room, his nails scraping against the wooden floor, seeming deafening in the closed quarters.

He stopped behind the chair at the end of the table, lifting those huge, pawlike hands and curling them around the top. His nails were so long and sharp. Like daggers.

"You are afraid," his voice rumbled out, and I felt it in every part of my body. "I can smell the sweet sweat on you, hear your breathing pick up."

I didn't respond. I couldn't.

"No harm shall come to you. That is not why you are here."

Oh, I knew why I was here. I didn't think he would hurt me, but sometimes death wasn't always the worst fate.

He cocked his head to the side slightly as if

examining me, as if I were the one so unusual he was having a hard time grasping that *he* was in *my* presence.

The movement of his head inclining had his thick hair moving over his shoulder. I could see his slightly pointed ears, watching as they twitched, which caused my heart to beat wildly.

"Woman," he growled. "I can hear your heart racing. I told you there was nothing to fear from me." He slowly slid his hands off the back of the chair, his nails scraping the wood ominously before he started walking around the table and closer to me.

This in turn had me moving to the other side, our steps parallel; the only thing stopping him from getting to me was the slab of wood that suddenly seemed wholly inadequate.

He gripped the back of the chair at the head of the table, situated right in front of the fireplace, pulled it out, and sat his heavy form in it.

He dwarfed that massive thronelike structure, leaning back so the wood creaked from his substantial weight. The firelight caught the sharp points of his horns as they arched up and backward.

"Sit," he growled.

His voice sounded so monstrous, all guttural and

harsh, that a small sound left me and I stumbled back so quickly I nearly lost my footing and had to reach out and grip the edge of the table to steady myself.

But I obeyed. I sat down across from him and realized how grossly I'd underestimated the size of the table.

At first I thought the table had seemed grand and long, enough distance separating us so that when we sat, I could still feel like I had control and safety.

But as I sat down on one end and he on the other, I realized how close we really were. So close I smelled the wolf, the primal scent that clung to him.

To occupy myself, or perhaps as a distraction from the situation, I glanced down at the large silver platter situated at the place setting in front of me.

I could hear the Beast lifting his dome, metal banging against metal so loudly I actually glanced up.

He tossed the lid aside like some kind of heathen who couldn't be bothered with formalities, then glanced down at the entire roasted chicken before him. He lifted his gaze to mine as if he felt me watching him, and his lower tusks became more prominent as he bared his teeth.

Was that supposed to be a semblance of a smile?

At the startled sound that left me, he scolded and gestured a large paw toward me, presumably to open my lid, too.

Maybe he wanted my approval at dinner, which seemed unbelievable, but I did what he said.

I raised my fingers, trying to stop the shaking in them, and gripped the top, lifting it and instantly inundated with the scent of rosemary and butter, roasted herbs and onion. I set the lid on the table, seeing another whole chicken before me.

At least five potatoes had been cut up amidst carrots and celery and placed around the meat.

This was more food than I'd ever seen in a sitting. And certainly nothing that I could ever finish on my own.

"Is it to your liking?" he growled out.

I looked up at him, slowly dragging my tongue along my bottom lip before pulling the flesh between my teeth. I didn't miss how he glanced down to watch the act. He slammed his hands down on the table, his expression showing frustration as his head lowered, his gaze still watching my mouth.

His nails dug into the wood, creating gouges that sounded so loud I pressed my back to the chair, trying to make myself as small as possible as a fearful noise left me.

His growls grew louder, and as if he caught himself, he pulled his nails out of the wood and cleared his throat. For a second he didn't move, didn't make a sound, and kept his focus off of me.

"Eat," he finally said and ran his paw over his face and fangs. His chest was rising and falling as he looked down at his platter, his beastly, bushy eyebrows pulling down low as he stared at his food.

He didn't wait for me to obey before he tore into his own food.

I felt my eyes widen and my mouth go slack, and I couldn't stop watching as he devoured his food. And that was exactly what I was witnessing.

There was nothing formal or delicate, noble or human, in the way he ate. His paws and claws were swift as he picked up the chicken and tore at the meat with his sharp teeth, growling and snarling as if he were ravenous.

Meat was flying everywhere as he shoved it in his mouth, then he attacked the vegetables, potatoes, and pieces of carrots and onion scattered around the tabletop, covering his face and all of his fur.

I concealed my mouth with a hand and kept

watching him, but when he glanced up and saw my undoubtedly horrified look, he froze. After looking down at the platter, then at my untouched one, then back into my eyes, I felt a strange sort of amusement spring to life in me.

"I, ugh," he said in that strange, deeply distorted voice of his. He ran the back of his paw over his mouth and reached for his wine goblet, guzzling it so fiercely the ruby-red liquid dribbled down his hairy chin and chest.

I burst out laughing then, unable to stop the humor I found in this very unconventional situation.

"I'm sorry," I finally said and wiped the tears from my eyes. "I've just never seen anyone be so ravenous—" My words stilled when he suddenly stood, looked at me ferociously, then stormed off.

I sat there alone, feeling all kinds of shame that I'd clearly humiliated and offended him. The instinctual part of me pushed forward, and I was about to stand and go to him, when I heard a crash and ear-splitting growl that seemed to shake the entire castle.

So I stayed right where I was because I really didn't want to approach the Beast when I was the one who'd just pissed him off.

CHAPTER
FOUR

Beast

I didn't pretend I had not acted irrational at dinner the night before as Belle had laughed at me while I ate.

But for the first time in my life I had felt... humiliation.

As she looked at me with tears of amusement streaming down her cheeks, her perfect, small pink mouth split into a smile, I had realized how ghastly she probably thought I was.

I had looked down at my platter, food scattered all over the table, down my shirt, and covering my face. It had been so long since I had company, since I had eaten with anyone, that it had not even occurred to me that I had zero etiquette.

And Belle had witnessed all of that, probably seeing me as disgusting.

Instead of acting like a grown male, I stormed out of the room, destroyed the hallway wall with my claws, breaking several vases and throwing what Madame liked to call a "temper tantrum" along the way.

For two days, I had stayed away from Belle, shame making me watch her from the shadows and only allowing myself small glimpses of her as we ate dinner, which I forced her to do.

I had felt her watching me while I ate, knowing she was probably waiting for me to act like the primal creature I was. But I had been learning to behave as I stared at her slyly as she ate.

I watched how she dabbed her mouth with a linen napkin between dainty bites. I copied these acts and hoped that she would see I wasn't as demonic as the villagers saw me... how she probably saw me.

I kept to the back corridors of the castle as I followed her scent. I could pick up the locations of the staff throughout the castle, who every day would leave at suppertime, allowing me alone time with Belle.

Even if we did not speak at dinner and I left as soon as we were finished, I loved just being in her presence. I could look at her and never get tired of the inner peace she brought to me.

That was when I knew she would be all mine, when I saw her for the first time in the village and felt a *shifting* in me.

Did she know how often I had followed her, learned her likes and dislikes before I had found a way to make her mine?

Did she know there were countless times when I stayed in the shadows and watched her come to and from the village market just as the sun was setting?

I had learned to be good at hiding, good at not being seen by the villagers and hearing them scream as they saw me, or ran in the other direction as they crossed themselves as if their god would save them.

And then I watched her through the window of her small cottage as she made a pot of stew over the fire and ate by herself most nights. That alone was enough for me to want to slaughter her father.

How could anyone leave such a sweet, innocent, and beautiful woman by herself?

I would not have been above kidnapping her and

keeping her locked in my tower. But then the opportunity arose to essentially purchase Belle in the form of repaying her father's debt.

And I had taken it, shamelessly.

I continued to follow the corridor, the walls on either side of me littered with gouge marks from my claws, pieces of broken vases on the floor, and light sconces hanging from their wires.

I had forbid the staff from coming to this part of the castle, deeming this my wing to do with as I pleased.

When I entered my chambers, I headed to the large window that overlooked the gardens. I had heard Madame speaking with Belle just moments before, my ears twitching as the soft melody of my new wife's voice came up from the lower level.

She had asked for seed to feed the birds, at which point Madame had given her a filled satchel and sent her in the direction of the gardens.

And that was where she was now, standing amongst the roses that were in full bloom, a brisk breeze twisting the mauve cloak around her legs.

My pretty human was thick and round and so curvy that my cock had been hard just from thoughts of her. I pictured myself violently tearing her dress away with my claws, mindful of her perfect vulnerable skin.

I envisioned her standing before me completely nude, the fantasy painting a vivid image in my mind. She had thick thighs, wide hips, a soft, rounded belly, and tits large enough to feel substantial in my paws.

And her nipples—hard and colored a dusky rose —had my mouth watering. I wanted to run my fangs over them and bury my hairy, too-ugly face between them.

My tail whipped back and forth as my excitement rose, and I pictured running the tip along her body before parting her thighs and spanking her pussy with it.

I knew she was too beautiful for the likes of a creature like me, but regardless she was mine and I was not letting her go.

The stench of decaying roses filled my chambers, the vase with the desiccated flowers on the table by the window looking as lifeless as I had felt before Belle became mine.

Frustrated with myself and my lack of control, I swung my arm out and knocked the vase off the table, ceramic crashing on the floor, dead flowers and petals mixing with the shards.

If Madame had seen me, she would once again tell me I was acting like a "child." She was the only human who spoke to me in such a way. Anyone else I would have eviscerated for such an affront.

Huffing out another exasperated breath, I looked out the window and stared at Belle. Instantly I felt a little of my inner rage dissipate.

She was just so soft, pretty, and fragile to my brutality. I had always lived my life alone, the only companionship being my staff. And having Belle here made me feel... alive.

But being alone worked. It was easier that way, less judgment, less staring and speculation, rumors and fear.

For long moments, I did nothing but stare at Belle, appreciating her human complexity, the strength she showed me with her laughter, even though I knew she was afraid. She took this situation that was forced upon her and made the best of it.

My cock was hard, throbbing, the front of my trews already damp from the copious amounts of pre-cum seeping from the tip.

I should not have loosened the top.

I certainly should not have reached in and curled

my paw around the thick, ribbed flesh and pulled it out.

And I really should not have thanked Mother Nature for causing a breeze that blew at the perfect moment, which caused the skirting of her dress to sweep up her thick, creamy thighs so they were on clear display.

I growled low and slammed a paw on the windowsill so hard the wood cracked from the force. My breathing increased as my pleasure grew.

The smile on Belle's face as she found pleasure feeding the birds turned me on, and I felt the thick, copious amount of seed seeping from my cock and falling onto the floor.

I ran my palm over the head, growling at how good that felt, smearing my cum around and making my cock slick as I jerked off.

The sound of it dripping was obscene but made me growl as I got even more aroused.

I ran my big, meaty hand over the girthy length, mindful of my claws as I stroked myself.

The ridges around my shaft grew harder, filling with blood. I imagined thrusting into her and making Belle take every heavy inch, knowing it would hurt her, but picturing her crying out and clutching me, telling me she couldn't take anymore.

But I would not be able to stop. She'd feel too good, and in return, I would bring her pleasures she had never dreamed of until soon she would be telling me *not* to stop.

I ran my thumb over the nodule at the top of my cock head, knowing the firm piece of tissue would become harder and rub her from the inside out, reaching hidden places until she came all over me, gushing on me and making a mess the same way I would when I got off.

I grunted and groaned, growling louder, one of my paws curled around the windowsill frame, my claws tearing at the wood, splinters digging into my flesh.

The entire time I stared at Belle, watching as she slowly stood and started sprinkling seed on the grass, as she bent over and her plump, round ass was in perfect view.

I would fuck her there too, part those plump cheeks, lick and spit on her asshole, getting it all nice and wet before I made sure to spray my cum on the tight entrance. I *needed* her primed for my cock, so she would be covered in seed by the time I slid in deep.

My dick swelled even further, a thicker rib in the center of my length expanding and filling with blood. Once I was deep in her, the center of my cock would swell to the point I'd be locked inside. The knotting mechanism would ensure my cum stayed deep inside of her and took in her womb.

With that image in mind, I growled so loud the window shook from the force and I came, hot, thick jets of my milky white cum spraying the wall and floor, my balls so full of my seed that my orgasm made a puddle on the ground, dripping from the slit at the tip.

Those ridges that ran around my cock pulsed, causing even more cum to pump out.

Belle glanced over at the castle, her gaze finding the window from which I watched her.

She would not be able to see me from the distance, but I looked into her face, my body giving a big shudder as the last ounce of my semen spurted out of me and made a big mess on the floor at my feet.

My barreled chest rose and fell harshly as I caught my breath, my focus never leaving Belle as I watched her gather her things and head inside.

My tail whipped back and forth, sexual agitation filling me once more because coming hadn't eased my need in the slightest.

I could not hold back from claiming her for

much longer. I could not be gentle or soft and sweet like she deserved.

I was very much the monster and animal she saw before her.

Maybe being soft or gentle and giving her space wasn't the right move. Maybe she needed to see that my desire for her was a living, breathing animal within me?

Perhaps she needed the dominance of my touch and words to bring her to me?

And the sooner I claimed, marked, and knotted her, the sooner she would be filled with my seed and grow big with my young.

And then she would be irrevocably mine.

CHAPTER
FIVE

Belle

I'd walked the countless corridors, snooping into various rooms.

I touched every vase, ran my finger down every picture frame, and walked the halls over and over again. I was starting to lose my mind.

It had been days upon days that I'd been at the Beast's castle, and the heavy loneliness was starting to weigh down on me. And although I was used to being by myself, this place was different. It was too grand, too vast.

I only saw the Beast at dinner, where he required me to eat with him nightly. And I was starting to look forward to those moments.

Because as the days passed and I would stare at him across the table, I started to see he wasn't as frightening as I had first assumed.

Sure, he was massive and scary in appearance, with his hairy, animal-like body and his horns and fangs, his hands that weren't really hands at all. And I wasn't ashamed to admit I'd thought about what they'd feel like touching me.

Was his fur soft or coarse?

Could he be gentle touching me with those deadly claws?

More and more, I thought about such things, my curiosity rising as I caught myself staring at him for long moments over the dining room table.

I didn't think about my father much, because I knew whether I was there or not, his life would still be the same. He would live it exactly as he had, probably still gambling, going into debt, and not thinking about how I was.

I found myself wandering into the kitchen, where I could hear pots and pans banging and Cook shouting in French to Sous Chef.

Because I didn't know the names of anyone aside from Madame and Pierre, I'd gotten used to just calling them by their household titles. They didn't seem to care—that was, if they bothered to address me.

I stood in the entrance of the kitchen and glanced around the corner, seeing Cook, a robust man with a shock of white hair, a big potbelly; rosy, rounded cheeks, and the most sour expression on his face that made you second-guess approaching him.

Sous Chef was the complete opposite physically, a willowy man with long dark hair he kept in a braid that hung down the center of his back. He had a milky white complexion, bushy dark eyebrows, and the most infectious laugh I'd ever heard.

Despite Cook's terse words and sour attitude, I'd seen them joking, and whatever Cook said could make Sous Chef laugh hysterically until he was doubled over and gripping his belly.

I watched as Cook pulled out two roasted game hens and started displaying them on silver platters. Then Sous Chef finished dressing the platters as Cook prepared dessert, which I could see was a homemade peach cobbler with fresh whipped cream.

I turned away before they saw me, before Cook scolded me for snooping. I often wondered if Cook liked the dinners to be a surprise, or if he just had a perpetual attitude.

I started aimlessly walking around again, having a little bit of time to kill before I was supposed to meet the Beast for dinner. I stopped and looked at a landscape painting, the brush strokes precise, the color vivid.

A smile tugged at my lips as I felt this warmth fill me. I wondered if Beast had done this, and I laughed softly because I couldn't see such a big monster painting something so delicate. And then I felt unfair and bitchy to think such an awful thought.

He hadn't hurt me, hadn't purposefully frightened me. My fear seemed for the unknown and his visage, which he couldn't help.

I was so lost in looking at all the paintings that it wasn't until I felt a tingling on the back of my neck that I realized I wasn't alone.

I looked over my shoulder and for a second didn't see anything, but then my gaze landed on a darkened corridor that forked off of the hallway. It was there that I saw the glowing eyes of the Beast, his huge body filling up the entryway, his shoulders nearly touching the edges of the doorway, his head having to be cocked to the side so his horns didn't take out the top of the frame.

His eyes positively glowed this otherworldly shade, a red hue that seemed to illuminate the small space before him.

I couldn't see his visage very well, just the overall shape, and the very clear fact he was staring right at me.

I expected to feel the familiar hesitancy I'd gotten when I saw him. But as I stood there, I didn't feel anything but this warmth that filled me. I even found myself taking a step closer, could see his face more clearly when my eyes adjusted to the darkness.

His nostrils flared when I took another step closer, then one more until we were just feet from each other. I had to crane my head back to look into his face, the Beast stationary, yet his focus never wavered from me.

I started breathing harder but couldn't place what I was feeling. It was definitely curiosity, but I didn't feel any fear or disgust. In fact, I felt a tightening in my belly, a flutter in my chest.

And I didn't realize I was lifting my hand until it was in front of me and my fingers were an inch from his wide, barreled chest, half of the buttons of his shirt undone as if he had been too impatient to finish.

His chest was so hairy that the shirt couldn't

contain all the dark, thick fur. And once again, I wondered if it was soft or coarse.

"My female," he growled out in that rumbled, deep voice of his.

Maybe I should have been more concerned at those two words, at the thick possessiveness laced within them. But I'd be lying if I didn't admit it had a thrill moving through me.

"Touch me. Take your fill, ease your curiosity." I didn't think I'd ever get used to his inhumane voice, but... I liked it.

And I was just about to place my hand on the center of his chest, let my fingers run across all that fur, when I heard a loud clatter come from the kitchen followed by Cook cursing. I curled my fingers into my palm, blinked back to reality, and took a step back.

The Beast looked behind me into the kitchen, growling ominously, dangerously. It had me shivering, which had nothing to do with fear. I felt an unusual warmth settling between my thighs instead, and clenched my legs together. But all that did was add more pressure and had me sucking in a sharp breath.

He huffed out, the act so primal and animal-like that it reminded me of when I'd walk by the stables and heard the stallions stomping their hooves and breathing out through their noses in frustration.

I took a step back and the Beast took one forward, the movement feeling very hunter-and-prey like. Again I felt more heat, more wetness between my thighs, watched as his nostrils flared, and heard him inhale deeply.

And I realized he could scent me. And I knew he liked it.

I kept backing up and he kept moving forward until I felt the wall stop my retreat. But I realized I wasn't escaping, I wasn't running away from him. I liked him prowling closer, invading my personal space, his body heat potent as it swirled around me.

The scent of the wilderness clung to his fur—a mixture of pine needles, fresh air, and hints of sunshine. But underneath that fragrance was something deeper and darker, a musky aroma that tingled in the back of my nose and made me feel all sorts of ways that confused me.

"Eat your fill at dinner tonight, Belle."

The Beast's voice sounded extra growly, and I felt it skate across my bare skin, his gaze flickering across my collarbones and lower still until he was staring at my cleavage that couldn't be contained by the bodice of the gown.

Although the material molded to my form perfectly, fitting me like a second skin, it didn't hide the lushness of my womanly body.

"Because you'll need your energy when, after supper, I require my new wife to bathe me."

And with that, he lifted his hand, one black, deadly looking claw coming closer to my face before he gently wrapped a curl around it.

The ringlet molded around one of his big fingers, then he lifted his hand to bring the strand to his nose, inhaling deeply as he rumbled out in a low tenor.

And I felt that vibration right between my thighs again. He made that wondrous noise before letting the curl fall back against my cheek.

He stared into my eyes once more, just a moment longer, before he took a step back, holding his arm out for me, and waited until I slipped my hand in the crook of his elbow.

And only when I did that did he lead us into the dining room.

But all I could think about was what we would be doing afterward.

CHAPTER
SIX

Belle

Iwas pretty sure I'd been standing here staring at the cloth in my hand for the last five minutes.

I felt like I didn't know what I was doing, even though this was the most natural thing in the world.

But I could feel his gaze on me, felt his body heat surrounding me, and especially smelled the most potent, primal scent that came from him.

After dinner, he led me out of the dining room, up the staircase, and into a grand bathing chamber.

Porcelain and tile surrounded the walls and flooring, with a pedestal basin, a clawfoot tub, and fresh oils and dried petals in apothecary jars sitting on a small stool making everything seem softer, like I wasn't about to bathe the Beast.

"Wash me, wife."

I shivered at the sound of his growly, inhuman voice. It was harsh and deep, rough, and sounded almost demonic.

I walked over to him as he started undressing. I kept my gaze firmly straight ahead when his shirt came off; then, when he removed his trousers, I closed my eyes as overwhelming, warring emotions filled me.

My hands shook as I forced myself to open my eyes once more and move toward the Beast.

I dipped the cloth in the basin of warm, soapy water, then started cleaning his forearm. He was hairy all over, but I was surprised at the downy softness as my fingers skated over it.

A low, deep rhythmic purr came from his chest as I moved the cloth up to his bicep, over his bulging shoulder, and brought it back down.

I could feel his focus on me, an intense stare that made me acutely aware of our size difference.

My head barely came up to the center of his chest, and although I was thick and lush, a woman who had a curvy body, the Beast made me feel positively dainty.

I tried to clear my mind and not take note that although the Beast was big and burly and so not human, he was also beautiful in a strange, fantastical way.

I glanced up and looked at the big, arching swoops of his horns as they curved back from his forehead. They were textured and thick, and before I knew what I was doing, I was running the cloth over one of the horns.

His body visibly tensed, then he shook and the purring grew louder, more pronounced and mixed with a growly tenor. I should have pulled my hand away, stopped touching his horn, but it felt so good to touch him.

"When I first arrived, Madame said you chose well. What did she mean?" My voice was low as I ran the cloth over his massive, hairy forearm once more. When he didn't answer, I looked up at him from under my lashes.

He watched me with hooded, red, glowing eyes, his unearthly appearance frightening yet causing this tingle of something else to move within me, to settle right between my thighs. "I learned about you, as much as I could, having

Pierre gather information on your likes and dislikes."

I paused and glanced into his face.

"I learned you enjoy romance stories."

My breath hitched, even though he said those words with a cool, calm tone.

"So I made sure to get any and all romance novels I could get my paws on in the five kingdoms."

My heart was racing so fast, and I found myself holding my breath as I absorbed his confession.

"But if you want more, I will get you whatever you desire. I just yearn for you to be happy here... with me."

I felt the betrayal of tears pricking my eyes but blinked them back.

This is wrong. It is wrong to feel anything but fear and disgust toward the Beast.

He was big and scary, but I found this strange sort of beauty in how he was created, in the words he spoke.

"I saw you in the village. Knew I'd take you as my wife." His words were sometimes hard to decipher because of his fangs, but I'd heard those loud and clear. "And so I wanted to win you over. But fate worked in our favor this time, because here you are. Mine."

I shivered again at the lone word, how it made me feel... everywhere.

"Keep washing, darling." His voice was low and hypnotic.

The cloth rested on his forearm, and then I was back in the present and staring at his huge erection, the member standing straight and hard between us.

All soft words he'd spoken pushed to the back, I felt my arousal rise again. I'd done a good job of not looking when he'd gotten undressed, but there was no ignoring *that*.

His cock was as thick and long as my forearm, with the same downy dark hair starting right above it and spreading up to his hard, defined abdomen.

I might have been virginal, but I knew what a human male had between his legs, and what the Beast had certainly wasn't that.

The head was a flared crown with a prominent slit at the end. And at the top of the tip, there was what looked like a hard nodule. My mind raced with how that would feel inside, pressing against all kinds of hidden places.

Copious amounts of thick white seed were steadily dripping from the slit, falling to his hairy, muscular thighs and dripping to the floor. I couldn't believe how much there was, given the fact I didn't believe he'd had an orgasm.

If there was this much before he got off, how much came out when he found his pleasure?

The shaft was so girthy I involuntarily clenched my thighs, knowing it would take *work* to fit that all inside a woman.

He had what appeared to be a ribbed definition going all the way around the length, and once again all I could think about was what it would feel like inside of me.

I felt my eyes widen as even more thick, white seed spilled from the crown, as if he heard my thoughts and found pleasure from them. And when I heard him inhale, I snapped my gaze up to his face.

"It'll feel like nothing you've ever experienced before," he growled out and leaned in, bringing our faces closer together. His tail whipped back and forth, reminding me of when a cat was focused, ready to pounce. "I'll fill you up to the brim, make you feel like you'll split in two."

A vibrating growl left him.

"And when you don't think you can take any more, I'll shove even more into you until we both come and I fill you so full of my seed that I'll get you big and swollen with my young. And when I pull out, my cum will pour from you." His nostrils flared as he inhaled, growling again as if pleased with my scent. "And after that, I'll breed with you over and over again until I'm sure your womb is filled with all of me and there's no doubt you'll give me heirs."

I was shocked and embarrassed, my face burning, my heart racing.

"How dare you talk to me in such a manner?" The words sounded flat to me, and when he grinned, his fangs and tusks predatory and flashing, I knew he didn't feel the heat behind my words either.

He made a noncommittal noise deep within his chest before saying, "Explore me as you wish. Learn how your husband is made just as I will learn how your body is formed, your curves and the lusciousness that makes you... you."

I felt his voice deep within my body, my inner muscles in that hidden spot between my thighs clenching.

Never had I thought such scandalous things, images of him and how he'd hover over me with that huge body rutting between my thighs. And, God, he'd take his pleasure as animalistic as he did everything else.

The sounds he'd make...

I didn't know why all of that turned me on as much as it did, but I visibly shivered in response.

His groan told me it hadn't gone unnoticed.

I tried to keep a more clinical approach on washing him, trying not to look at all the different parts that made him so different and so very male.

I swallowed a large lump that suddenly formed in my throat as I ran the cloth up and down his fiercely corded forearm, back up his bicep, and over his shoulder.

I could see the muscles underneath flexing and held my breath, realizing that trying to keep this completely clinical was so not working.

I lifted his heavy arm up and ran the cloth between each of his fingers, taking note of the soft pads on each one.

They were reminiscent of how cats were formed, and when I gently pressed on the center of one, a small gasp left me when his already elongated claw came out a little bit more.

Although he said nothing, his body so still and tight, I could feel him watching me. I ran the cloth over his chest, periodically dipping it in the warm, soapy water before moving it back.

His fur became wet, his male nipples becoming

visible underneath. Hard and shaped like coins. My inner muscles clenched once more.

I started washing lower, the hard ridges of his abdomen contracting from my touch.

Before I went too low and saw too much, I moved back up and started washing his other arm, then his shoulder, and along his other horn.

"So good, wife," he rumbled out.

My heart hiccuped in my chest as I washed his face and ran the warm, wet rag along his brow.

I focused on his nose, even though I wanted to look into his eyes. The bridge was flat and wide, his nostrils flaring as he inhaled sharply and exhaled just as harsh.

Although his mouth was full, it looked slightly distorted because of his fangs and tusks. He even had a seam starting in the center of his upper lip and connecting with his nose, which was so very feline.

His brow was prominent, and when I looked into his eyes, his expression was so intense I felt it down to my marrow.

I heard and then felt the cloth drop from my hands, splashing into the basin of water beside me.

I murmured my apologies and felt my face heat on fire. There was another low rumble from him, which I was starting to realize meant he was pleased.

Exhaling slowly and closing my eyes, I reached into the basin of water to scoop out the cloth.

"Wash my legs, wife."

I felt a tingle move throughout me and I opened my eyes, which was a horrible mistake seeing as I was right in line with his massive, long, and completely foreign-looking erection.

Although he would fit, I, of course, could only think about how I would be stretched to the brim, and he would split me in two, as he so eloquently put it.

I'm an adult. Treat the situation as such.

"Wash *all* of me, Belle."

The way he said my name was so husky that I was ashamed when the soft moan left me.

I snapped my focus to his face, noticing the way his eyes flickered from red to the normal deep brown I'd seen so far.

We held each other's gaze for long seconds, but I knew it was because I was terrified that... I might like it.

"Go on," he taunted.

I licked my lips, his gaze dripping to watch the

act at the same time, wet the cloth once more, held my breath, and ran it along his lower abdomen.

I spent an ungodly amount of time washing the same flat, hard expanse of his stomach, and when I heard a deep chuckle come from him, I narrowed my eyes that he thought my embarrassment was funny.

So, while staring into his red, glowing eyes, I wrapped my cloth-covered hand around his erection. His grunt had a sharp slap of pleasure and pride filling me. The fact that I affected him this way gave me my own pleasure.

I dragged the rag up and down his length, my fingers unable to wrap fully around his girth, the feeling of his hardened ridges prominent under the strip of fabric.

"That's it," he purred. "My good girl."

I sucked in a sharp breath at hearing that praise. I dragged my hand back down his length, felt the hard protrusion at the tip and found myself glancing down, transfixed at watching as I stroked him.

I twisted my wrist so I could get a better look at him, my pussy clenching and growing wetter as I ran the tip of my thumb over that nodule right at the crown.

He groaned and thrust his hips forward, pushing more of that monstrous erection into my palm.

I moved my hand back down, pulling at the foreskin so the bulbous head and seeping slit were revealed. I stroked back toward the tip, watching, fascinated, as his foreskin moved back in place.

But his cock was so big, so thick, that I could still see the slit, watching as cum steadily dripped from him, landing on his thighs, catching in all that thick, dark fur.

"My good, good girl likes to watch what she does to me, and likes to see all the seed I give her."

Breathing harder, I didn't dare respond. I couldn't have found the words to respond anyway.

I stopped, but a low growl left him and, a second later, he wrapped that oversized paw around my hand, keeping me right where I was... with my fingers wrapped around his length.

"Don't stop." It was a demand, and when I looked up at him, the Beast started using the pressure he had on my hand to stroke himself.

He moved so aggressively, more than I ever would have dared, twisting my hand at the crown, running my fingers over that hard protrusion before making sure to get my palm slick and sloppy with his dripping seed.

My mouth parted as I sucked in a sharp breath when he slammed his free hand on the wall beside his head, crushing the plaster, bits and pieces falling to the ground.

I found myself getting turned on as I watched those black claws digging deeper and deeper into the wall. I felt his other hand tightening around mine to the point it slightly hurt but then felt insanely good.

The Beast was pumping both of our hands fast and hard against his shaft, every once in a while curling my palm over the slick tip. I was amazed at how much semen was coming out of him, a steady stream falling from the tip.

His big, hairy balls were swaying from the force of jerking him off, those twin weights swinging freely beneath the length. And all the while he stared at me, his gaze so penetrating it felt as if he were actually touching my pussy.

"Do you see that, wife?" He growled, and I felt my eyes grow even wider in shock as more cum spilled out. "That's all for you." He grunted when my hand moved over the crown before sliding back down the length and squeezing tightly at the base. "I'm going to fill you up with it, shove this big cock deep in you, make you take every last ounce until it's pouring out of you so that when I pull out of your cunt, it'll hurt so good."

I gasped, knowing I should have felt scandalous hearing these vulgar, obscene words. But I felt a trickle of wetness slipping down my inner thigh, felt my pulse beating wildly at my center.

"I'm going to keep giving it to you, over and over again, not stopping until I fill your womb so full of my seed that it takes deep inside of you, and you grow big and heavy with my young."

I clenched my thighs together, which added pressure to my clit, pulling a moan from me. And that was when I saw his entire body tense, and heard his claws dig so deep into the plaster they were now like black holes.

"That's it, wife. Make me come. Watch as it goes everywhere because you made me feel so good."

My gaze was locked on his cock as he stroked himself using my hand. He did this three more times before stilling, my palm wrapped around the center of the heavy length, and I felt something grow thicker, harder, right under my hold.

It had even more wetness spilling down my inner thighs as I watched him orgasm.

And he came so much, so forcefully, that his seed sprayed along the wall, covering the floor in thick, hot jets of milky ropes that shocked and aroused me.

After a long moment, he huffed out and sagged forward, a paw still dug into the wall.

"You see the mess you made me make?"

I snapped my focus up to him, feeling dazed and slightly confused by what I just witnessed.

And a whole lot of aroused.

He stared at me with a hooded expression, his eyes still glowing that otherworldly red.

His hold on my hand loosened and I took a step back, unable to look away from his massive cock that was still semi-hard and still dripping semen.

"I can't wait until you're mine in all ways, Belle."

I jerked my focus up to his face, holding my breath as he slowly smiled, the visage distorted because of his fangs and tusks. But I was starting to find it not ugly or frightening.

In fact, I felt that familiar pulse between my thighs again *because of it*.

His nostrils flared and he took a step closer, his big, heavy cock bobbing, his large, hairy balls swinging back and forth from the movement. He lowered his head slightly, the massive arches of his horns turning me on.

Oh, God... what is wrong with me?

"And I know you can't wait until you're mine as

well. I can smell the sweet honey that flows out of that tight little cunt right now."

I took another step back just as I felt my pussy become even wetter.

"And once you are in my bed, I will brand you until you smell of my seed, sweat, and musk. It will cover every inch of you from the inside out, and be so deep in your womb that there will be no denying you are mine."

CHAPTER SEVEN

Belle

I felt like something had shifted in me after the washing encounter with the Beast.

It had only been a day since we shared that experience, but it had been all I was able to think about.

In my mind, I kept envisioning my hand sliding over his powerful, inhuman body. I even found myself throbbing between my thighs, had reached down and touched my soaking wet slit when I made my way back into my room last night.

Biting my lip as those memories crowded my mind, I remembered how good it had felt. But there had been something missing, and as I felt my orgasm claim me in the darkness, I knew what was missing.

The Beast should have been the one who was stroking me, who had brought me to climax.

I'd been wandering in the hallways, forcing myself not to seek him out because I was afraid of myself around him, terrified of how I was feeling.

Leaning against the wall, I rested my head back and closed my eyes as I thought about the vulgar, obscene things he said. I grew wet all over again as the images of the lewd things I witnessed played on repeat in my mind.

I opened my eyes and stared across the foyer, lifting a hand and touching the center of my throat, feeling my pulse beating rapidly.

I felt warm and wet and soft all over at the very thought of just submitting myself to the sexual whims of the Beast.

I wanted depravity. I craved to see what it would be like—feel like—to just lie in the center of the Beast's bed naked and spread out and let him have his filthy way with me.

"Oh, God, I'm losing my mind."

"Miss Belle?"

The sound of my name being called had me pacing to the side and seeing a slender woman in livery attire standing at the entrance of the foyer, holding a letter in her hand.

"Mail for you, Miss." She held it out to me and I smoothed my hands along my skirting, walking forward and taking the envelope. I gave her a thankful smile.

The young woman was gone before I could say anything else, and I glanced down at the envelope to see it was from my father.

My heart was racing as I tore into it with anxious fingers, unfolded the paper, and started reading the almost illegible text.

My dearest daughter, I've come into trouble. I would humbly beg that you ask for help from your husband. I know this comes at an inopportune time giving your recent nuptials, but if I don't get help, I fear, my dear Belle, this may be the last time we ever speak. I need money. A lot of it. Please meet me tonight at the village south entrance, and bring your beastly husband as he's the only one who can help. I'll wait for you in hopes you come to my aid.

For a second I didn't move, just kept reading the letter over and over again until finally my fingers curled around the paper on their own until it was nothing but a ball in my palm.

The truth of the matter was—I shouldn't feel any kind of obligation to help my father. He'd tossed me aside to save his own hide, and he hadn't even bothered to check up on me since.

He didn't care about how I felt in the slightest. He didn't ask how I was doing, or if I fared well. He didn't ask if I was happy.

No, he'd immediately wanted something from me.

I was angry and hurt, but my anger took a front seat despite an errant tear slipping down my cheek.

I shouldn't have thought anymore about it, yet I found myself moving through the house in search of one of the staff that could lead me to where the Beast was.

I ended up finding Madame in the kitchen. She was with the young woman who'd given me the letter. They were folding linen napkins when they spotted me and stopped. Madame gave me a soft smile when I held out the crumpled letter.

"I need to speak with the Beast."

She glanced at the letter, then at the young

woman, before giving me a small nod. "Master can be found in his study. Upper level, third room on the left. Would you like me to show you?"

I shook my head, murmured my thanks, and then I was leaving, heading up the stairs and into the room she directed.

When I stood on the other side of the massive double oak doors, I lifted my hand but hesitated to knock.

I glanced down at the crumpled-up letter again. Once more asking myself why I was doing any of this. Why did I care? But at the end of the day, he was my father.

My only family.

If I didn't help him, it would make me no better to him than a stranger.

"Come in, wife," the Beast called out before I even knocked on the door.

My hand shook as I reached out and turned the handle, pushing the heavy wood inward before stepping inside.

For a moment, I was taken aback by the interior. Everything was dark wood with engraved accents. There was a massive desk with a roaring fire behind it, and bookshelves lining three out of four of the walls.

The Beast stood by the fireplace, the cloak he wore making him seem even larger, which seemed unbelievable.

"How did you know I was out there before I even made myself known?" The question didn't really matter, nor did his answer. I was stalling from the real reason I was here.

The Beast looked over his shoulder at me. The flames from the fireplace, coupled with the fact this room didn't have a single window to let in sunlight, gave it all lowlights and eerie shadows.

"I'll always know where you're at, Belle. I can sense you in any part of the castle. I can *smell* the sweet scent that surrounds you."

My face heated at his words because they seemed so very intimate, and then when I thought that, the memories of what we shared last night came back to mind.

He turned and faced me, and I told myself not to look, but still I glanced down at his trews, seeing he was already hardening, as if my very presence was an aphrodisiac.

His gaze flickered to the crumpled-up paper in my hand, and I looked down to stare at it, loosening my fingers around the edges.

"My father sent a letter," I said almost absentmindedly. "He's asked for help." I lifted my head and stared at the Beast. "From you. Monetary help. Of course." I swallowed harshly, feeling embarrassment that I was asking the Beast for this.

It didn't matter if we were legally husband and wife. I'd only been here for such a short time.

And the shame that my father continuously got himself into these messes, and that I was the one who bailed him out, had my face heating and had me glancing down to the ground in humiliation.

When I felt his finger under my chin, lifting my head up, I stared into his eyes.

We didn't say anything for long moments, but the low humming sound he made could've been interpreted in many ways.

Pleasure. Empathy. Displeasure.

"I'm sorry," I found myself saying, and if the Beast's expression could soften, I felt like it would've in that moment.

He cupped the side of my face, his palm so big that one could easily cover my entire head.

It wasn't lost on me every time I was near him that the Beast could break me as if I were nothing but a toothpick between his teeth, snapping me in half until I was but a splinter.

"My father's troubles aren't your concern but—"

"He's your family. Your only family." He smoothed a claw gently along my jawline. "That was the past, though. You have me now. So if he needs help, that's an extension of you and I'll gladly step in. Because I care for you."

I felt my belly tighten, my heart skip a beat. How could this Beast, so big and fearsome, be gentle and soft? How could he completely go against everything I'd ever heard about him?

Was he just misunderstood or was he this gentle only with me?

I cupped the back of his palm, my hand so insubstantial compared to his, his fur so soft beneath my touch.

I smoothed my thumb over his prominent knuckles, could feel his body visibly shiver, and heard a deep sound leave him. Because of me.

"I will leave momentarily. I will fix whatever wrongs he's done that directly affect you."

"I'll go with you," I said instantly but he was already shaking his head.

"I would prefer you stay here, in the safety of the castle. I will not put you at risk."

I felt a smile curve my lips. "But I have you to protect me."

He growled low and moved his hand to curl it

around my nape. "You are my only priority. I will protect you until it kills me."

I felt that flush of heat move through me, that warm wetness between my thighs once more.

I let my gaze move around his face, memorizing every dip and hollow, everything that had once been unusual to me but now seemed fantastically beautiful. I stared at his mouth, so foreign yet so attractive.

I actually found myself taking a step forward, placing my hands on his furry chest, feeling his muscles and sinew clench and relax against my touch.

He didn't say anything but he started breathing faster and harder as I lifted up on my toes, bringing us closer together.

As if he knew where my thoughts were going, he lowered his head at the same time I tipped mine back.

"You're not what I expected," I whispered, our mouth so close together that my bottom lip almost touched his tusks.

"You are everything I envisioned." His words were a deep rumble that I felt all the way down to my toes.

He still had his paw around my nape, the gentle

prick of his claws against the side of my throat reminding me how very deadly he was. But I knew without a shadow of a doubt, deep within my soul, that he'd never hurt me.

He would always keep me safe. And with that thought in mind, I gently pressed my mouth to his and gave the Beast my first kiss.

He groaned deeply but didn't kiss me back, just held still as he let me explore his mouth. I ran my tongue along his bottom lip, then over one tusk before dragging it up and touching the point.

He growled anew, and I felt his paw tighten around the back of my neck as he pulled me in closer, my breasts smashed to his chest, my nipples painfully hard.

He was panting against my mouth, his lips slightly parted as I tentatively pressed my tongue inside, exploring him, touching mine with his.

He tasted spicy like cinnamon. So wild and potent that I couldn't stop the moan that was pulled from me. And then he was tilting his head to the side and crushing his mouth harder to mine.

He moved his tongue along mine and I was shocked to feel it was textured, rough like a feline's.

The kiss wasn't gentle or soft. It was slightly

awkward given his fangs and tusks, but God, it felt so good. And he tasted even better.

He broke away far too soon, but he didn't pull away and instead ran his big, fat, textured tongue down my cheek, along my jawline, and down my neck.

I gasped at how strange it felt, the warm wetness of him literally licking me.

He did this back and forth, up and down the side of my neck, bathing me in this very primal way before he kissed me once more. I opened wide, my mouth far too small to fit well against his, but it didn't matter. It all felt so good.

He dragged his tongue over my lips before plunging it inside, pulling out and repeating the action.

But all too soon, he pulled away. I leaned forward, staring up at him with no doubt a dazed expression. I curled my fingers tighter into his fur, pulling him toward me, aching for more.

He groaned and smoothed a thick pad along my bottom lip. "If I don't stop, I'll take you here right now, Belle."

My pussy clenched and I felt more wetness coat my lips and smear along my inner thighs. He inhaled sharply. I knew he smelled me, my arousal.

"And I want you in my bed, spread and soaked—that juicy cunt all primed for me—when I fuck you for the first time." He growled. "But after that first time..." His eyes flashed red. "I will fuck you in every single room in the castle, marking you with my scent so it saturates the air."

I clenched my thighs together and bit my lip.

"But make no mistake, I want to fuck you and fuck you hard and thoroughly. I ache to fill every hole you have. I *need* you to be covered in my cum so you smell like me all over."

He took a step back and focused on my breasts, which were heaving beneath my bodice.

"I want to fuck you between those huge tits, Belle. I want my cum to cover your neck, am feral with the desire to smear it all over you and make you taste me."

I closed my eyes at his obscene words, feeling dizzy.

I forced my eyes open to see his eyes flashing red.

"I can smell how wet your pussy is for me."

I sucked in a startled breath.

"Leave and go get ready." The Beast's voice was harsh as he turned from me. "If you don't leave right now, I'm liable to tear off that gown, spread your thighs, and fuck your cunt hard and rough like the animal I am."

I only stood there for a second, but then he turned back around and growled. He took a step forward, his head lowering, his gaze still trained on me. A part of me wanted to stay right where I was, to see how far I could push him.

But I wasn't a fool. I couldn't do this right now. No matter how much I desired to see how beastly my new husband was.

CHAPTER
EIGHT

Belle

The sun was barely starting to set over the horizon when the Beast helped me up on a massive steed and climbed up behind me.

He'd tried getting me to stay back again, but I'd insisted, too worried about what my father was going through if he was in that much trouble. I knew enough about Gaston that the man was evil to the bone, and I had no doubt he would torture my father just for the hell of it. I had to do everything in my power to help, even if this was foolish of me.

The stallion huffed and stomped as I gripped the reins. I blew out a slow stream of breath when the

Beast placed a paw over my belly, pulling me back against the hardness of his chest.

I felt so dainty against him, his palm nearly covering me from breast to pelvic bone, his thighs as thick as my torso and framing either side of me. I'd never felt safer.

I glanced over my shoulder and tipped my head back so I could look into his face. He was already watching me. I hardly knew the Beast, had only been here for such a short time, yet inexplicably I trusted him.

It wasn't like he hadn't told me not to come. I didn't listen, so I had to take responsibility for my own actions. And that meant I needed to be strong in the face of my fear of the uncertainty of what we were about to ride into.

"I would prefer you stayed." When I didn't respond, he gave me a semblance of a smile. "As I thought," he murmured. "I will protect you," he said and tightened his hand against my belly.

I faced forward, nodding even though I wasn't looking at him anymore. And then we were off, the stallion picking up speed the farther we got from the castle.

We were a couple of miles away, deep into the

woods, the sun already having fully set when the wind decided to pick up.

I tightened my cloak, securing the hood over my face better, but I worried about the Beast. I glanced over at him and saw he was focused in front of us, his expression fierce and powerful. He didn't seem like he cared at all about the inclement weather.

He was also wholly desirable.

When did my fear for his unusual physique shift and change into something erotic and beautiful?

I had to face forward and close my eyes, taking a deep breath so I didn't get aroused all over again.

The last thing I needed was to tempt him because he would be able to smell me.

But maybe he did sense my desire because I felt something along my leg and glanced down to see the Beast's tail wrapped around my calf. It wasn't tight, but it was secure, and strangely enough, I felt like it was an act of possessiveness.

I stared at his tail, at the sleek, silky fur that covered it and the tuft of darker fur at the end. My thoughts turned loud as I imagined him running it along my naked body.

I lowered my head and gritted my teeth, trying to act like I had control of myself. I heard the sound of a wolf howling, knew we were getting close to the village border, and my anxiety rose.

I hadn't questioned why my father wanted to meet there instead of at our cottage. I just assumed he needed ambiguity, his shame too strong to let anyone else see him begging for help, especially from the Beast.

I saw the wall of the village, an imposing structure of wooden planks and pointed tops with burning torches on each end.

The closer we got, the clearer I spotted my father standing out to the side, his short, stout figure cloaked in heavy wool, the hood up, his movements antsy as he paced back and forth.

The Beast pulled the steed to a stop a short distance away from where my father paced. I could feel how tense my new husband was behind me, his paw like a vise around my abdomen.

"What's wrong?" I whispered, feeling my own anxiousness rise at his response to the situation.

He growled and I looked around, feeling the hairs on the back of my neck stand on end. Something felt off but I couldn't place it. I didn't see or hear anything aside from my father slowly making his way toward us, the leaves and twigs cracking under his boots.

But when the Beast started growling louder, I held my breath and braced myself.

"Belle?" my father said, and I was about to get off the saddle when the Beast made a low sound of disapproval and pulled me harder against his chest.

"I didn't think you would come," my father said softly, and now that he was close enough I could see him eyeing the Beast warily although I found it strange seeing as he asked for my husband to come with me.

"You find me so heartless as to not help?"

He shook his head. "Of course not. It's just after everything..." He glanced at the Beast before looking back at me. "Anyway, thank you for helping me." He addressed my husband, who still sat tense behind me, not responding.

I still felt the tightening on the back of my neck, the hair on my arms standing on end. "Something's wrong," I said more to myself but the words came out regardless, echoing all around me.

It was only a heartbeat after I spoke those words that the Beast growled louder, and a second later we were thrown off the stallion.

I braced myself for impact, but the Beast twisted just before we crashed to the forest ground, taking the brunt of the force, my back landing on his chest.

I heard the Beast roar out a second before someone grabbed my hair and I was dragged off suddenly. Whoever held my hair tugged so hard I cried out in pain.

My ears stung as I lifted my hands to grip the fingers that dug into my scalp, hoping to ease some of the pain and pressure.

I was tossed aside, the air leaving me roughly. I pushed myself up quickly, and that was when I saw several men with torches and pitchforks raised in the air, charging after the Beast.

Oh, God. It was an ambush.

My husband stood before them like the very devil himself. He ripped off the cloak, tore at his shirt until it fluttered in tattered pieces to the ground, and then he was tipping his head back and roaring so loud the leaves above shook.

The moonlight highlighted his horns and powerful physique, and if I didn't know how gentle he could be with me, I'd have screamed in terror and escaped.

"I'm sorry. I'm sorry."

I could hear my father repeating that apology over and over again and spotted him off to the side standing next to... Gaston, who had an evil gleam in his eyes, a sadistic smirk on his lips, and stared at the Beast as if he wanted so much blood until he was coated in it.

"What have you done?" I whispered but neither man paid attention, the growls and roars of the Beast mixing with the shouts and curses of the villagers who continued to attack him.

"The Beast needs to be taken out. He needs to be eradicated and rid of this world. He's evil and is nothing but a corruption. He doesn't deserve the wealth he has. He doesn't deserve you, Belle. I'm going to fix that, though. I'm the man—" Gaston shouted as he pounded his chest like a barbarian "—who's going to be the hero of this story."

The Beast roared out again and I focused on my husband. When one of them charged forward, the Beast flung him away as easily as if he were an annoying fly.

But then another threw a pitchfork, the prongs sticking into his furry body before he gave a rage-filled growl and ripped it out, flinging it back to the man. I heard the human men screaming in pain, pitchforks sticking out of their bodies, the scent of blood coating the air.

Gaston made an angry sound. I heard a revolver being drawn. I looked over my shoulder to see Gaston holding the gleaming metal in his hand.

Bodies were littered around, the men who attacked now nothing more than corpses on the forest ground.

The Beast's chest was rising and falling, his broad, massive shoulders and chest so wide he blocked out anything else behind him. Although it was fairly dark and I couldn't see much, I could see he had wounds and could smell the coppery tang of blood in the air.

"You," the Beast snarled and lifted a huge furry arm to point a deadly black claw at my father. I watched in awe as that claw grew a little longer, became a little sharper. "Leave before I tear out your trachea for putting Belle in danger."

I felt dizzy as I snapped my focus to my father. He didn't even look at me as he hightailed it in the other direction. I lifted a hand to my chest, feeling that last shred of familial love fade. He'd left me, didn't even check to see if I was okay.

I knew this was the last time I'd see him, and strangely enough... it felt like a weight had been lifted off my shoulders.

"And you," the Beast growled so menacingly at Gaston that I shivered in response, hearing the nocturnal animals scurrying away as fast as their little legs could take them.

"I'm going to make sure your death is slow and painful, satisfying my bloodlust and delivering your heart in my palm to my female."

The Beast took a step forward, and I swore everything happened in slow motion as Gaston took aim. I didn't even realize I was moving until I was running toward Gaston.

I heard the Beast roar out, then the cracking bang of the revolver going off before I was shoved to the side.

I quickly checked to make sure I hadn't been shot—in too much shock to let it sink in—but when I realized I was unharmed, I glanced back at where the two males stood off to the side.

Gaston didn't have time to shoot again, not when the Beast was already charging forward and gripping him around his meaty neck and lifting him off the ground.

He grabbed Gaston's wrist that held the revolver, lifted it high in the air and, with a sickening crack, broke the bone. The weapon fell to the ground and Gaston howled in pain.

"I am going to enjoy this, especially with my female watching me slay the ones who would have hurt her, who put her in danger."

I should have stopped the Beast, maybe pleaded

to let Gaston live. But I said nothing. None of the men who attacked the Beast deserved to live.

I felt my stomach clench when the Beast plunged his fist into Gaston's chest, breaking through his ribcage, pulled out his heart, and held it in his palm as if it were nothing but a piece of fruit.

He dropped Gaston to the ground, his lifeless body crumpling as if a rag doll. Then my monstrous husband turned to face me and held out his arm, presenting Gaston's bloody heart to me.

"Beast," I whispered, knowing I should feel fear, but I felt something darker, something dangerous, that filled my blood and made me hot.

He dropped that organ to the ground, lowered his head and flared his nostrils, and he inhaled... as he scented the wetness that was steadily coating that intimate spot between my thighs.

The Beast was panting as we faced off, my father long gone after the warning, Gaston and the others nothing but corpses around us.

"Run, Belle," he growled. "Run as fast as you can, because when I catch you—and I will—I am going to fuck you so hard there will be no doubt who you belong to."

I didn't need any other warning. I turned and ran.

CHAPTER
NINE

Beast

I could have been sightless and I still would have found her.

I inhaled deeply, taking in the scent of her anxiousness, her anticipation, her... arousal. Belle wanted me to chase her, was needy for me to be the hunter and her the prey.

And that was exactly what I was as I tore through the forest, swiping at the trunks of trees with my claws, splitting them in half.

I felt the blood pumping through my veins faster and harder as the anticipation and excitement of catching her filled me.

My muscles swelled, and my cock got thicker in

preparation for claiming her, of parting her thighs and forcing myself deep inside her tight heat. I anticipated filling her up with my cum and making her womb grow with my child.

I impatiently tore at my trews, rendering material and letting it fall to the forest floor. I growled low when my cock was freed, pre-cum already a steady flow out the tip.

I felt most in my element right now, a beastly creature with nothing but nature and wilderness covering me as I chased down my prey.

I had given her a head start, and could easily catch her right now, but I stayed back, watching as she weaved in and out through the trees, periodically looking over her shoulder at me.

I got harder, more aroused chasing her like this. I could hear her harsh breathing, her slight inhalation as she sucked in a breath when she saw I was right behind her.

So close I could sense the salty sweat that dotted her brow, could smell the adrenaline seeping out of her pores, and could all but taste the sweet honey that spilled from her cunt.

I reached a paw out and gripped the laces of her dress, tearing at them until the material opened in two parts. Her silky smooth back was revealed, and I growled in pleasure.

She cried out, and it wasn't a cry of fear but of excitement.

"Run faster, little rabbit. I can smell your sweet, honey-coated pussy."

In a move faster than she would ever be able to contemplate, I tore at her dress. She cried out then moaned but lost her footing, falling forward. I grabbed her waist and spun her around, pressing her onto the moss-covered ground and bracing my paws on either side of her head.

She was curvy with a womanly body, all thick thighs, a nice rounded belly, and breasts that were large and supple. Her nipples were a deep shade of red and hard from the chilly air, and my mouth watered for a taste.

"I'm going to devour you." I gripped both of her wrists and lifted her arms above her head, then leaned back and used my other paw to force her legs open.

Her scent surrounded me instantly, and my body swayed as I leaned in and ran my face over her belly then lower still to her mound. She smelled incredible, all musky sweetness and *mine*.

My tail whipped back and forth and I dragged

the tip over one of her legs and back down to curl it around her ankle, pulling her leg open even wider.

She lay still for me, panting, her mouth parted as she stared at me with all the desire consuming her.

"I want you to tell me that you are mine, and to admit you will surrender in all ways."

She squeezed her hands tightly into fists, but I still kept them above her head, looking down at her stretched-out body, taking in all the perfect, beautiful dips and hollows that made her extraordinarily beautiful.

"Be my good girl and answer me. Tell your beastly husband that you know you are mine in all ways." I leaned in and ran my nose along the edge of her face, down the side of her throat, and kept descending as I scented her.

"I don't know what changed," she panted and opened her eyes, but they were barely parted, just opened enough to let me see her desire reflected back at me.

I allowed myself to scent her, moving back up the center of her chest, between her breasts, and was still as I inhaled deeply. "Mmm, so sweet I could eat you alive." I pulled back and watched as her breasts shook from her forceful breathing.

The aroma of her soaked pussy had my cock

jerking and leaking copious amounts of cum, dripping between her thighs.

I wanted to rub all that seed into her flesh, make her smell like me until she was marked as mine and mine alone.

My focus was trained on the sight of those twin fleshy mounds shaking as she gave me a soft, sweet moan.

"I see myself as yours, Beast."

I leaned back even more so I could really get a good look at her, and let my tail slide along her inner thigh, the furry tip teasing that soft junction where her cunt and leg met. She gasped and tried to close her legs, and I growled out a warning.

"You are going to lie there and take what I give you like a good girl." She licked her lips and I was riveted to the sight.

"Yes."

"Tell me why." My voice was guttural, harsh, and so inhuman I did not know if she could even hear me clearly.

"Because I want you to fuck your wife... to claim me in the primal way you desire."

To reward her, I leaned forward, keeping my gaze latched on hers, and spit on her pussy, letting the saliva prime her already soaked cunt.

She squirmed and groaned, and I pulled back and grinned a no-doubt terrifying visage of one, and brought the tip of my tail down on her swollen cunt.

"Ahhh," she cried out and arched her back, her big tits bouncing from the sudden force.

"Be still and let your monster of a husband spank this little pussy." I brought my tail down again, over and over on her soaked folds at the same time I let go of her thigh and moved my paw up the center of her chest and circled her slender throat.

I added pressure to her neck as I kept swatting her pussy, making sure I spanked her clit harder each time I brought it down.

She thrashed her head back and forth as I grew feral with the need to sink deep in her cunt, to make her stretched, to hear her cry out because I was far too big for her to take comfortably.

"Please," she cried out. "Please, Beast. I don't know if I can take much more."

I had my face right by hers then, our mouths close enough that my tusks nearly touched each side of her jaw. "You will take every single thing I have to give, and when you think you can't take any more, you will beg me not to stop."

I ran my tongue along her lips, over her jaw, along her cheeks, and licked her like the fiend I was.

I lapped at her throat, inhaling her scent in the process because I couldn't get enough.

My cock was a leaking faucet of cum, my seed smearing all over her thighs, my cock throbbing with need. The tissue in the center of my shaft throbbed, just waiting to be buried in her pussy so it could swell and knot inside of her, keeping us locked so she was forced to take my cum.

I hummed in approval, letting my tail slither along her belly, the tip teasing her nipples. I smacked those tips until they were hard and wet, the hair at the end of my tail wet from her cunt juices.

I brought the tip to my nose and ran the end under my nostrils, smelling the musky scent of her need for me. "I want to fuck you right here on the dirty ground, with the moon above us, the cool forest air around us, and your cries of pleasure filling my ears."

When I looked between her thighs, I saw she was lifting her hips, as if she were silently begging me to fuck her. And I would, like the nasty fucking creature I was.

I leaned forward and gripped her behind her knees, brought her legs up to press to her chest, and stared at how pink and spread open her pussy was for me.

And then I spit on her cunt again right before I leaned in and started licking at her juicy folds.

Although she was drenched, her pussy cream dripping down the crease of her ass, Belle needed to be good and sloppy for when I finally fucked her.

My cock was too long, too thick and big, and she would need all the help she could get taking every last inch.

My fangs and tusks and the overall size of my face made it hard to do much else but lick her cleft and clit. I wanted to get in there nice and deep, suck that bundle of nerves at the apex of her thighs and feel her quiver and come for me.

But she was far too small and tender for the likes of the primal fucking I wanted. My sweet, soft human wife needed me to be gentle this first time.

So I got my fill as much as I could, her moans and the way she ground her cunt against my mouth having my cock kick and my big balls draw up. I was so full, so ready to fill her up.

I moved a little lower so I could drag my tongue along her tight asshole, her pussy cream having slipped down the crease to coat the tight ring of muscle. I pressed my tongue into her, forcing it inside of her sweet, supple body, feeling her squeeze the muscle.

I grunted, made harsh sounds that vibrated her ass, and when she reached out and gripped my horns, I groaned so loud a few birds startled overhead. I licked and licked and licked her asshole, so feverish for her I needed my little female now.

"Ah, my sweet Belle, I cannot wait until I am in your tight heat and you are sucking me dry, milking all my seed out because you are hungry for it."

I broke the suction I had on her ass and started licking her thighs, alternating between her legs, lapping at her soft flesh, unable to get enough.

I was so hungry for her as I drew my large, textured tongue over her mound, along her soft belly, dipping it into her navel before moving up and sucking her nipples into my mouth again.

I couldn't get enough of these twin, tight beads as I let my fangs gently scrape along them, feeling them tighten up further. I pulled back long enough to see that I left marks, bruises that looked pretty on her skin and were another branding that had the animalistic side of me roaring out in triumph.

I was so fucking hard at the sight of our differences. She had soft, peach-colored skin and a tiny, smooth face with big eyes, a pert nose, and full lips. She was curvy but still so much smaller than me.

And here I was, an ugly monster covered in dark fur still getting the beauty. I may have fangs and tusks sprouting from my mouth, making it impossible to kiss her properly, or even eat her sweet cunt out as thoroughly as I wanted, but I'd make sure she was well pleased.

And I'd ensure that I fucked her well, by claiming my human wife over and over again until she walked bowlegged and her pussy was sore from my huge cock plowing it.

I wrapped my tail loosely around her throat to keep her in place as I flattened my tongue and dragged it up her chin and over her lips before plunging it in her mouth. I repeated this action over and over again until she had her back arched and her tits pressed against my chest.

The kiss was sloppy and wet, so noisy it was like two wild animals rutting in the darkened forest.

"I need..." Her voice was breathy, barely audible.

"I know what you need." I leaned back on my hind legs and gripped the heavy base of my cock, stroking myself from root to tip, squeezing out thick ropes of cum so it dripped out and covered her pussy.

While staring at her face, I continued to stroke myself as I moved my tail back down between her thighs and teased her clit. She lifted up on her elbows, staring down the length of her body at what I was doing to her.

"Beast," she whispered but her words were cut off when I started teasing her opening with the tip of my tail before slowly pushing it in.

Her jaw went slack and her head tipped back as if she didn't have the strength to hold it up any longer. I moved my thumb along the bundle of nerves to the top of her pussy, rubbing it back and forth, all the while masturbating like a dirty fiend.

"Come for me, Belle. Give this monster the pleasure of watching you come unhinged." I pushed my tail deeper in her, feeling her pussy muscles clamp down on it. "Come on, darling. Give it all to me." I curled the tip of my tail upward, teasing that walnut-sized bundle inside of her at the same time I added more pressure to her clit.

I snarled and pumped my fist faster over my cock as she seized up beneath me and gave me what I wanted.

Her hands went to her hair as she tugged the strands and orgasmed.

My focus was riveted to her cunt, her pussy hole

filled with my tail, her folds covered in cum from my leaking cock. And when she squirted, clear fluid spraying from that pretty pussy and covering the base of my tail and tops of my thighs, I came, too.

I grunted and growled as my seed made a mess all over her, and when she gasped and I felt her pussy muscles tighten again on my tail, feeling her climax again, my entire body shook with ecstasy.

Cum poured out of me and I caught it in my paw, filling my palm with the hot, thick seed before looking back at my wife. "Open for me, sweetheart."

She was panting as she parted her lips further and obeyed me so well. Cum overflowed my paw as I brought it to her mouth, seed dribbling onto her belly and breasts, her neck and chin. I reached out with my free paw and gripped her jaw, forcing her to open wider for me as I tipped my palm and poured all that cum into her waiting mouth.

"Swallow all of it. You are not going to waste one drop, darling."

Her moan was low and long as she drank all of the seed I had to give her, reaching up and catching droplets that slipped from her lips. She brought those fingers back to her mouth and sucked them clean.

"My good girl," I purred.

My cock was still hard and ready to breed her. I shifted back down and ran my furry cheeks and jaw all over the tops of her thighs. I let my saliva spill from my mouth as I kept rubbing myself on her, wanting every single part of me *on* her.

I purred as I kept rubbing my face over her belly and higher until her tits were smeared with her wetness as well as the scent of my cum and spit, branding her.

I slammed my paws on either side of her head, gouged my claws into the dirt, and dug my hind legs into the earth so that when I was buried to the balls in her body, I'd *really* get in there *deep*.

She was so tiny beneath me, all pink, tender skin, a vulnerable human body, and the most gorgeous thing I'd ever witnessed as she stared up at me with wide eyes and a parted mouth.

"Open up for me like a good girl," I growled, unable to close my mouth fully because my fangs were too long, too sharp. "Head to the side. Let me see that pretty throat."

She moaned and tipped her head back, baring the side of her neck. My mouth watered, my jaw ached. And then I was striking like a cobra, sinking my teeth into her, giving her my mark.

This was nothing but a superficial, primal, and

animalistic need in me. Her wound would heal, but I would do it all over again. Every fucking time I was buried balls deep in her tight cunt, I would mark her.

I would hold her tight enough she had bruises on her arms and legs so that anyone who saw her would know that she was mine.

They would be able to smell me on her, see my possession on her creamy flesh, and know she was loved well, fucked thoroughly and regularly, and that she was *mine* above all else.

I broke the bite and looked down at the twin open wounds on her throat. I rubbed my cheeks across that bite, smearing the blood on both of us. I smelled the coppery tang of it in my nose, and lifted a paw to wipe my face, rubbing it all over my fur.

Fuck, that smelled good. And tasted even better when I ran my tongue over my lips, lapping at the blood, her pussy cream, and the clean taste of her asshole after eating her out.

"I hope you are ready," I said in a distorted voice against the shell of her ear. "Because even if you have second thoughts, you are mine, sweet girl. Forever."

"Yes," she breathed, her voice husky.

"Reach down and grab my huge cock, place it at

your cunt, and then hold on because I am going to fuck you until you can't see straight."

I felt her fingers tremble as she shoved her hand between our bodies, took hold of my leaking cock, and placed the knobby head at her hole then slowly pushed in, taking her virginity, before slowly pulling out.

I breathed out a shuddering breath as I felt the tight, wet heat of her cunt. "Now grab my horns like a good girl. Stroke them like they were my cock and you were desperate for me to get off."

She reached up without preamble and gripped the base of my horns, and my entire body shuddered at how fucking good that felt.

I moved my tail along her thigh, curling it around her ankle for a second before slipping it between our bodies and teasing her asshole with the tip once again.

"Look at how small you are, so fragile compared to me." I thrust into her and she cried out. "So tiny and weak, frail in comparison, taking a monster cock like you were made for it."

She made the sweetest mewls, the loudest cries for me to never stop. "I need more. Never stop. Never."

"Oh I won't, sweet girl. I'll fuck you over and

over again until I get you pregnant. I'll never stop even after that, making you take all my cum, covering your body with it so you grow addicted for it every fucking night."

She wasn't speaking, but kept making noises that turned me on even more, made me even more wild in my frenzied need.

I thrust the tip of my tail into her ass, braced my paws on either side of her body, dug my back claws into the earth, and started throwing my hips back and forth, unable to give her gentle, sweet, and soft.

I fucked her savagely, not thinking of anything but getting us off, of my pleasure and breeding with her. I was running on pure instinct now, and nothing else mattered except the sweet scent of my female's arousal.

"Give me one more, let me feel that cunt milking me because your body is hungry for more of what only I can give you."

"Yesss," she moaned and it was her orgasm that set off my own.

I slammed into her once, twice, three times, and on the fourth, I buried every inch of my ribbed shaft in her, feeling my knot start to thicken, my big hairy balls starting to tighten close to my body with my impending orgasm.

"Beast," she screamed as her climax peaked again, and that was my undoing.

I threw my head back and roared.

I came and came and came so much I felt my seed spilling out, squirting out from where we were connected and coating our thighs and bellies.

"You're doing so good," I said huskily, shakily, as it was hard to even speak the words. "Making me come so hard." My voice was barely audible as she kept moving her palms up my horns until she was at the tips. Then she slid her hands back down, stroking them as if she were jerking me off.

"They're so thick and hard."

I groaned as my orgasm kept going on and on, a crescendo of pleasure and pain that I never wanted to end.

Having her touch my horns was like a direct line to my cock, an electrical current that made it all the more pleasurable.

I'd knotted inside of her, the center of my cock swelling to the point it was painful in the best fucking way as it ensured I was locked deep in her body.

"So good. You are doing so good, you feel so fucking good, my little human wife." Her pussy clamped around me again. "No one will ever make me feel so damn feral with desire, or make me come so fucking hard."

I was still pumping out spurts of seed, making sure her womb was filled, making sure there was no way she wouldn't carry my baby after tonight.

The sounds that came from me were inhuman, a testament to how far gone I was.

With my hands caging her in on either side of her body, my claws dug into the ground, dirt embedded underneath them, my focus landed on her shoulders, where I'd scratched her the hell up, those claw marks covering her pale skin. And then I looked at her throat, where my bite mark was nice and prominent.

A wave of possessiveness, of proprietary need, slammed into me, and I snarled and fucked her harder, having to hold her in place as I pounded into her soft, but tight pussy.

I leaned forward and dragged my tongue across that mark, over and over again, licking at the droplets of blood that beaded from the puncture wounds.

She tasted sweet and coppery. She tasted like mine.

My knot grew harder, the rising swelling even

more, teasing and pressing against the sensitive inner walls of her deliciously hot cunt.

It was long moments of me unable to pull out of her tight heat, not that I wanted to. I could've stayed buried deep in her body and never been happier. But when I felt the swelling of the knotting start to go down, I forced myself to pull out of her.

I groaned; she moaned and gasped.

I knew she had to be sore, and that had hard pleasure filling me all over again.

Right before I fully pulled out, I leaned back and looked down, humming in appreciation at the sight of her virgin blood all over my big, swollen cock.

"Say it," I demanded without looking up from between her thighs.

"I'm yours," she said without more prompting.

"Yeah, you are, my sweet, perfect girl." I pulled out that last inch, my thick cock head popping free of her swollen, soaked, and pink pussy.

I wanted nothing more than to plunge back inside. But the next best thing was keeping her gloriously thick thighs spread open so I could be a voyeur and watch as my cum poured out of her like a geyser.

Thick rivers of semen slipped out of her pussy

hole and slid down the crack of her ass to pool underneath her on the ground.

My cock ached painfully, and I could have fucked her all night, pounding into her over and over again as I kept filling her up. But I knew my small human wife was sore.

She needed rest, to recoup, and gather her strength for more of the rough fucking I had planned.

Besides... we had our entire lives for me to continue to devour her. And I hoped she was ready, because I didn't plan on ever stopping.

The fairy tales were wrong...

Beauty could want the Beast.

TEN

Belle

I was in this twilight sort of state as the Beast lifted me off the ground and held me close to his chest.

The soft touch of his mouth to the crown of my head as he gave me a gentle kiss did funny things to my heart.

When did I fall for this creature? How could I have fallen for him so quickly?

When did I realize that just because someone had an outwardly monstrous appearance didn't mean their inner selves were ghastly?

Because as I thought of my husband, felt him

hold me, took in his wild scent, all I felt was this warmth and safety in his arms.

The movement of him walking through the forest, holding me as he presumably went back to the castle, was enough to lull me into a dreamlike state.

The sweat had dried on my body, and I was sore between my thighs, so wet and sticky from the remnants of his orgasm and mine.

In fact, my entire body felt covered in his cum and marks, his primal bites and scratches. I found myself inhaling once again, taking in the scent of him because it felt like the most perfect thing in the world.

It felt like home, like this was where I was always meant to be.

"Thank you for protecting me," I murmured sleepily and burrowed deeper against him.

I felt him running the smooth side of one of his massive horns against my cheek, the sound of him scenting me loud and arousing and so very perfect.

"I will always protect you. You are my life, and without you there is no me."

Oh, my heart softened even more, became painful as it pounded harder and faster behind my ribcage.

Before I knew it, we were within the castle and he was striding up the stairs. I did nothing but let him carry me, his furry body so warm and big and soft that I felt my smile stay in place.

The sound of a door opening and closing roused me, and then cool satin touched my naked skin. I blinked open my eyes, a dim glow coming from a candelabra sitting on the nightstand beside the four-poster bed.

I shifted onto my side and watched as the Beast disappeared behind a doorway.

Staring at the candelabra, I noticed the wax dripping down the brass stem to the base, then glanced at the small table over by the big picture window. A beautiful array of long stem red roses sat within a glass vase, a few petals having fallen to lie on the lacquered top.

The sound of running water drew me out of my thoughts, and a second later the Beast was walking back toward me, pulling my focus from the flowers to my husband.

I marveled at his sheer size, at the way his muscles were visible under all that dark fur. The candlelight caught his impressive horns, and the flickering light and shadows would have made him seem almost frightening if I hadn't already known how gentle he could be with me.

His tail flicked back and forth behind him, and my face heated, my body tingling when I remembered what he'd done with that piece of his body as he fucked me in the forest.

I wasn't sure what he was doing until he was on his haunches beside the bed, his body still so big despite him crouched on the floor, and holding up a warm cloth.

A surprised gasp left me as he placed it between my thighs, the heat pulling a hiss from me because I was so sensitive.

"You don't have to—"

"Shhh, let me take care of my wife." He gently cleaned me up, and all the while he stared into my eyes. There was this almost softness washing over his expression as his eyes became hooded. "It pleases me to tend to you, to ensure I've taken care of you after I've fucked you."

Butterflies fluttered in my belly at his words, and despite the soreness I felt, desire licked at my body once more.

Once he was done cleaning me, he lay behind me and pulled me in close to his chest. His body was warm, all that fur like my own personal blanket as I snuggled in closer to him.

I turned in his arms and tipped my head back, looking up and into his face, tracing his horns and fangs, his tusks and feline-like flat nose with my gaze.

"You're beautiful." I murmured the truth.

"I am a monster, ghastly. I know this."

I was shaking my head before he finished. "You're fearsome and strong, protective and beautiful in my eyes."

He took in a deep breath and closed his eyes for a second. "Say it again." He opened his eyes, the color flashing red, and a growl laced his words.

I knew what he wanted, what he meant, and it wasn't sweet endearments falling from my lips. I shimmied up on the mattress so I could kiss him, then ran my tongue along his tusk, which pulled a groan from him.

His cock was hard as it pressed against me, seed already smearing along my leg.

"I'm yours," I whispered against his lips, never having spoken truer words than those.

He growled and I found myself on my back again with my beastly husband hovering over me.

"You are mine. Forever. Let anyone try and take

you from me, and they'll see how dangerous I truly am."

"I never want to be anywhere else."

He closed his eyes once more and his shoulders tensed. "One day I'll make you fall in love with me."

Oh my sweet, big brute of a husband. I cupped his cheek and sifted my fingers through his fur. "I'm already on my way there." My voice was whisper-soft, and his answer was a rough sound pulled from his throat as he parted my thighs and slid back into my deliciously sore body.

He opened me up and filled me to the brim.

And he did so for the rest of the night.

EPILOGUE

Belle

"Let me see that tight fucking hole, darling," the Beast snarled behind me. "Reach back and pull your cheeks apart."

I gasped and did as he said, bent over the plush couch in the library, my body sweaty and hot and so turned on I couldn't think straight. My pussy was soaked, my juices slipping down my inner thighs because I was so ready for him.

When I reached back and grabbed my ass cheeks, pulling them apart so wide I felt the hole open slightly, I heard my husband growl again behind me.

"That's it."

I cried out and my body jerked on its own when I felt a sharp sting on my asshole. I didn't have to look over my shoulder to know he was spanking my anus with his tail.

He did this three more times until the pain mixed with pleasure and I was begging him to fill me up. And that's when he came on my ass, coating the crease with all that hot, thick seed, making sure I was good and lubed for that huge dick.

I glanced at him once more to see him spitting on me, too, a long line of saliva trailing from his mouth a second before making contact with my hole.

"Oh, God, I can feel the nodule at the top," I gasp-moaned, and he growled as he pushed in an inch as soon as I let go of him.

I knew that firm piece of flesh would rub on that sensitive spot deep inside of me, knew that he'd make me come hard again, squirting so I got him all wet and sticky with my juices.

Pressing forward more, he ground out, "Look at you nice and spread for me." When he leaned back, I was rewarded with a slap between my thighs.

I moaned and arched my back involuntarily. I was filled to the brim with him, my skin feeling stretched tight around his shaft.

His ribbed shaft felt so good inside of me, and when he slid out, I couldn't stop the pained sound that slid from me.

"Wait," I whispered when I felt him buck in me.

"No, sweet girl. Your time to stop this is over. But you would not want to stop it anyway, isn't that right?"

"You're just so big and thick," I breathed

He groaned in pleasure, and I knew it was because he loved hearing me talk about the size of his cock. The Beast said nothing else as he pushed back into me, which had my eyes rolling back in my head. I bit my bottom lip hard enough I felt the skin open up and tasted the coppery tang of blood.

He had his paw curled around my throat and turned my head to the side, running the pad of his thumb over my bottom lip and smearing that blood. Then I watched in obscene pleasure when he brought it to his mouth and licked it off, before going back for another bead. He smeared that second droplet down the center of my back, right down the length of my spine.

"Say it," he demanded as he did a steady pumping in and out of me.

I was panting, unable to speak for long seconds

until he growled so loudly I gasped and started speaking, obeying him.

"Fuck me. Fuck me like the animal you are."

He hummed in approval and then groaned the words, "Good girl. That's my sweet girl." The Beast pulled out so the tip of his cock was lodged in me before shoving back inside so hard I was pushed up on the couch again.

My husband snarled and clamped a paw on my shoulder, digging his claws into my flesh until I felt my skin break open under his touch.

I made a needy sound and whispered, "Yes."

"You like that, don't you?"

I moaned again and nodded frantically.

"Yeah, you like this animal fucking you... hurting you."

I still had my head cocked to the side as I watched him glance down at where he was fucking me. The Beast started to pound into me faster and harder, his paw on my shoulder keeping me in place.

"This is going to be fast and hard. I cannot help myself tonight, not when your tight ass is clenching around my cock, your body begging me to fill it up."

I held on to the back of the settee as he had one paw gripped around my shoulder, the other one holding my waist, his claws pricking at my flesh.

He started fucking me again, the Beast pulling out so just the tip of his cock was lodged in my ass before he plunged back in. His big hairy balls slapped against my clit every time he forced himself back in. The sound of wet skin meeting wet skin filled the room obscenely.

The Beast went wild behind me, grunting and growling, snarling and cursing as he fucked my ass, yet I knew he was still holding back, still trying to be gentle with me to an extent because he worried he'd hurt me.

"Do you wanna get off, darling?"

I couldn't answer, just made these broken noises in the back of my throat.

"Yeah, my sweet little human wife wants me to rub her clit and make her come." He pushed into my ass extra slowly after those words. "Do you need me to do that, sweetheart?"

I was panting as I glanced over my shoulder at him, my vision blurry, the pleasure so intense I felt like I was disconnecting from reality.

Of course the pain was also there, the fullness, the stretch and burn. But it all existed as one until I felt myself finally nod in agreement.

He gave me that frightening, but extremely attractive visage of a smile. And then his big paw was between my thighs, his palm so massive it completely covered me from pelvic bone to the crease of my ass.

The Beast added pressure to my clit with the heel of his palm and that was all it took for me to explode around him.

My inner ass muscles clenched around his hardness, milking him, drawing out his orgasm.

And that was all he needed to find his release.

It was long after both of us found pleasure that I sagged against the back of the couch, sweat covering my body, my ass full of his seed.

He still cupped me possessively between the thighs, gently stroking me, the pad of one finger teasing my pussy hole, his touch gentle despite what we'd just done.

With a harsh groan, he pulled out of me and I felt all his cum start to slip from me. The Beast kept my cheeks spread open so he could watch, and rumbled out a sound of pure masculine approval that I loved hearing.

"I will never get tired of watching you spread open as my seed slips from your body."

And when the last ounce of his cum slipped out, only then did he gently turn me around, pick me up in his arms and carry me out of the library.

I rested against him and let him support my weight, my heart rate going back to a normal rhythm; that incredible burn and ache between my thighs was constant.

The Beast was insatiable, but then again so was I. Especially given my condition. It seemed being pregnant had my libido working overtime.

He set me on the edge of the sink in the bathroom as he went to run the water in the massive bathtub. I continued to marvel anew that he had modern, heated water that was pulled from the well. He'd afforded me this luxury after we found out I was carrying, not wanting me to wait for the staff to fill the tub with hot water.

It took a long moment for it to fill completely, the steam rising from the tub, the humidity filling the grand space.

Once the tub was filled, he was lifting me up and gently setting me in the center and climbing behind me. He pulled me back so I leaned against his chest, and I rested my head between his muscular pectoral muscles as he held me.

The Beast placed his palm on my rounded belly, gently rubbing my skin in slow circles. He did this frequently, touching my stomach as if he couldn't believe his baby grew inside of me, or leaning in and kissing the mound, even whispering in gruff words that I couldn't make out. But his tone was gentle, sweet, even.

I spread my legs with his nonverbal grunt, and hissed when he cleaned the most sensitive, intimate part of me. It shouldn't have turned me on after what we'd just done, but I found that heat moving through me regardless.

"Sit up, darling. Let me take care of you."

My body felt soft and pliant as I shifted forward. A moment later, I felt his big fingers in my hair, his claws so gentle as he lathered the shampoo in the strands and massaged my scalp.

The scent of lavender and vanilla from the shampoo filled my nose, and I sighed happily. I closed my eyes, leaning against one of his thickly muscled and furry thighs, just letting my husband tend to me.

"Once I have you nice and relaxed, I'm going to dry you off with the softest cloth, lay you upon our bed, and massage your entire body with that jasmine and orange oil you love so much."

I moaned. "Keep talking."

He laughed in a distorted sort of way, then smoothed those heavy palms over my shoulders and back down my arms, and took my hands in his. He gently rubbed each one of my fingers. He massaged me gently, as gently as he could with paws so powerful he could cut down tree trunks with a swipe of one hand.

And when I was loose and content, relaxed in every way possible, he ran his nose up the side of my throat, rumbled in pleasure, and was rinsing me off.

I let him control every aspect of this as he lifted me up, dried me off, and carried me to bed. And then he made due on that promise of a massage.

By the time he was finished, I was oiled up, my muscles loose, that delicious ache still present between my thighs, and ready to do nothing but cuddle with my big monster of a husband.

And he gave me exactly what I wanted as he got into bed and pulled me over so I was curled up on his lap, both of my legs draped over one of his hairy thighs.

I sifted my fingers through his chest fur and rested the side of my face in the crook of his neck. The heavy weight of his palm rested on my belly once more.

"You know you are mine?"

I closed my eyes and smiled.

"You know I'll never be the valiant knight in shining armor protecting your honor. I'll be the savage creature that tears apart anyone who so much as looks at you."

Those words would have put fear in anyone else. But to me, that had a dark sense of safety settling inside of me, growing into a garden that I'd forever take care of.

"Say it again for me, sweetheart."

I smiled. "I'm yours. Always."

He growled a pleased sound. "That's right. Because the Beast finally captured the Beauty's heart."

The End.